the Mean Girl MELTDOWN

the Mean Girl MELTDOWN

LINDSAY EYRE

ILLUSTRATED BY
SYDNEY HANSON

ARTHUR A. LEVINE BOOKS
AN IMPRINT OF SCHOLASTIC INC.

Library of Congress Cataloging-in-Publication Data

Eyre, Lindsay, author.
   The mean girl meltdown / Lindsay Eyre ; illustrated by Sydney Hanson. — First edition. pages cm — (Sylvie Scruggs)
   Summary: Fourth-grader Sylvie Scruggs is old enough to join her town's new junior ice-hockey team, and she is a really good skater, even if she does have a tendency to close her eyes when she shoots, but fifth-grader Jamie Redmond does not like younger kids on the team, and when someone starts pulling pranks on Sylvie she is convinced that Jamie is responsible — and she enlists the help of her friends to prove it and get even.
   ISBN 978-0-545-62029-1 (reinforced binding : alk. paper) — ISBN 978-0-545-62030-7 (pbk. : alk. paper) 1. Hockey stories. 2. Bullying — Juvenile fiction. 3. Practical jokes — Juvenile fiction. 4. Teamwork (Sports) — Juvenile fiction. 5. Friendship — Juvenile fiction. [1. Hockey — Fiction. 2. Bullying — Fiction. 3. Practical jokes — Fiction. 4. Teamwork (Sports) — Fiction. 5. Friendship — Fiction.] I. Hanson, Sydney, illustrator. II. Title.
   PZ7.1.E97Me 2015
   813.6—dc23
   [Fic]

                                                              2015010284

10 9 8 7 6 5 4 3 2 1   15 16 17 18 19
Printed in the U.S.A.   113
First edition, September 2015

Chapter 1

It was the bottom of the last inning of the championship game. My team, the Raging Bulls, was up against the Red-Hot Devils. The Red-Hot Devils were ahead 4–5. I was on second base, waiting for Kimberly Sacks, our best hitter, to come to bat. We had two outs already. If we got one more out, the game would be over — the whole season would be over — and my team would lose.

Sweat dripped down my forehead. My heart thundered in my eardrums. I'd never been in a championship game before. My team had never made it this far. But we were going to win. I knew it.

I crouched low as Kimberly walked to the plate. I glared at Jamie Redmond, the meanest pitcher in the league.

Kimberly got into position. She brought her bat up to her shoulder.

Jamie Redmond just stood there.

"Throw the ball already," I muttered as I inched away from second base.

Jamie whirled around suddenly and tossed the ball to the second baseman, but I was already back, my foot on the plate. *Too late,* I thought. *Ha ha.*

Kimberly got ready again. She looked like a statue of baseballness. My heart twittered. Kimberly was going to whack that ball so hard, it would be a homer, and she and I would fly into home plate for the victory. The score would be 6–5. The Raging Bulls would win!

Jamie threw. Kimberly swung.

She missed.

"Strike!" the umpire called.

"Ha!" the second baseman next to me shouted.

"That's okay, Kimberly!" I hollered. "Next one's yours!"

Jamie stomped her foot three times to show how awesome she was. Then she got back into position.

Kimberly raised her bat.

Jamie threw. Kimberly swung. Kimberly missed.

"Str–iiiiiiiike two!" the annoying umpire shouted.

Kimberly stepped up to the plate again. Revenge was written on her forehead. She was not going to strike out this time. Hands on my knees, I scootched a little ways toward third.

"Time-out!" Jamie shouted.

"Time-out?" I said. "Right now?"

Jamie waved at her infield to come closer. The second baseman gave me an I've-got-my-eye-on-you look and jogged up to Jamie, who had stepped off the mound. The first baseman, the third baseman, the shortstop, and the catcher joined them. They gathered in a huddle. Jamie was giving them instructions I couldn't hear. I scootched out a little farther.

When they were done, the second baseman walked back to his base. The others returned to their spots too. All except for Jamie. She was bending over her knees like there was a miniature lion on her shoe telling her a secret.

Kimberly was ready to hit again. Everyone else was waiting. "Come on already!" I shouted.

Jamie whirled around and chucked the ball toward me as hard as she could. The second baseman leaped into the air, caught the ball, and tagged me on the shoulder.

"Ow!" I shouted. "You can't do that! She wasn't back on the mound. It was still time out!"

"Totally legal," Jamie said, smirking a smirkity smirk.

"You're out!" the umpire called. "Game over! The Red-Hot Devils win!"

"Ump!" I cried. "That's not fair. The game hadn't started again!"

"What grade do you think she's in?" the second baseman asked Jamie.

"I don't know," Jamie said. "Maybe second or third. Watch — she'll probably start crying."

"I will not start crying!" I shouted. "And I'm in fourth grade next year. Fourth grade."

Jamie and her friend, her follower, her munion, were jumping around with their team, giving each other high fives like they'd just won the championship game.

My team came out on the field.

"I can't believe you fell for that," Harry said.

"We would have won," Sammy said.

"It was soooooooo close," Nehu added.

My mom, our coach, just looked at me with a sad smile and mouthed, "It's okay," which was a big fat lie.

Georgie, Miranda, and Josh ran over to me from the bleachers. "They pulled the classic the-pitcher-calls-time-out-to-psych-out-the-baseman trick," Georgie said. "I saw it coming."

"You did not see it coming," I said, because he thinks he knows everything about baseball and he does not.

"What an exciting game!" Miranda said. "I've never seen a game end without a final pitch."

"You were brave to try to steal third," a tiny boy said. I looked down at him. Way down. I recognized him from somewhere — Georgie's baseball team, I think. He was in first or second grade. "Too bad it didn't work," he said.

"It almost worked," Josh said as Jamie Redmond walked by with her bag over her shoulder.

"Yeah," Jamie said. "Too bad almost isn't enough."

"You just got lucky!" I shouted at her. "Plus you cheated! Next time, we'll beat the pants off you!"

"Thanks for the warning," she said. "But if we ever play again, I don't think I'll be the loser."

"Oh yeah?" I said, my fists on my hips. "Oh yeah?"

Jamie kept walking like I wasn't even shouting at her.

"Don't worry," Miranda said in her grown-up voice. "I'm sure you'll beat Jamie next year. Let's go back to my house and see if the cockroaches have molted yet."

"I'd like to see cockroaches molting," the tiny boy on Georgie's baseball team said. "Can I come?"

"No," I said, because I was too tired to deal with first graders.

Miranda grabbed my hand and dragged me over to the dugout. I didn't resist. We'd lost the championship! My team was mad at me. My friends were being way too nice. My mom was busy trying to convince my team that everyone can be a winner if they never give up, which was also a big fat lie. My twin brothers, Tate and Cale, were at my grandma's house, and my dad wasn't at my very first championship game ever, because he'd just won a big promotion at work and he had to go on a superimportant business trip. My body sagged with sadness.

Miranda helped me gather up my baseball stuff, and we started to walk home. I stopped for a moment to look at the field I wouldn't set foot on again for a whole entire year.

Last game of the season. The championship game. Lost. Because of me.

Next time, I promised myself, *you will win. And next time, no matter what, Jamie Redmond will lose.*

Chapter 2

Summer ended. September came. School started because it does that. And my mom finally, finally had her baby. We named her Ginny. She's cute, she's perfect, and she's noisy.

"You look tired," Miranda said to me one Monday in October. Georgie, Josh, Miranda, and I were at the back of our classroom putting away our backpacks.

"My dad came home from a trip at one o'clock in the morning," I said, sounding like a panther with a sore throat. "He woke Ginny up to give her a kiss, and she started to scream, which woke up the twins. Then the twins woke me up so I could say hello to Dad, and that woke up my mom."

"Oh no!" Miranda said, probably thinking of her nice, quiet house.

"It took forever to calm everyone down," I said. "And I had to get up extra-early to help the twins make their lunches, because my dad was too tired and that's supposed to be his job."

"Your dad makes really good lunches," Josh said, probably thinking of his mom, who does not.

"And then Tate and Cale decided to make sandwiches without bread again," I said, letting my head fall to my desk. "They just plop the peanut butter and jelly in a Baggie."

"Really?" Georgie said as if he might want to try that.

"Class!" my teacher, Ms. Bloomen, said. She clapped her hands. "Please take your seats. We have a visitor."

A tall, tall boy with dark, curly hair, dark skin, and a shirt that said DON'T MESS WITH ME — I KNOW SCIENCE stepped into the room.

"Ooo," Miranda whispered as we walked to our desks. Miranda loves science.

"This is Max," my teacher said. "He's a student from the high school. He is a Science Olympiad champion and you would all do well to look up to him."

Miranda nearly fell off her seat.

"He is also a hockey champion, and" — Ms. Bloomen sighed — "I believe that's why he's here today."

Hockey! Now I nearly fell off my seat. I love hockey!

"Thanks, Ms. Bloomen," Max said. "That is indeed why I'm here. We're starting a hockey league for kids in this area, and everyone in this room can sign up. The season will begin in two weeks, and, believe me, it will be awesome. Hockey is full of banging and hitting and scoring and shouting. But you wear lots of padding so you don't get hurt. We've got used equipment for you to borrow, so it won't cost much. Hockey is the best!"

"Well!" Ms. Bloomen said with a frown. "That does sound exciting. Everyone, raise your hand if you'd like more information about hockey."

I raised my hand high. My heart was thumping. My eyes felt sparkly. I was good at ice-skating. I was fast and I could do spins. My dad was a hockey champion when he was in high school, just like Max. He used to take me ice-skating on daddy dates, back when he wasn't so busy.

I looked at Josh, who slowly raised his hand. No other hands went up.

I gave Georgie a fierce look, the kind a jaguar might give a friend who was supposed to raise his hand and say he wanted to play hockey.

Georgie did not raise his hand.

I gave Miranda a nicer look, the kind a beetle might give its friend to encourage her to play hockey.

Miranda smiled back, but she did not raise her hand.

Max handed Josh and me hockey sign-up papers.

"They want to play too," I said, pointing at Georgie and Miranda.

Max gave both of them papers, even though they tried to give them back.

"And my dad can be the coach," I said. "He's great at hockey."

"Awesome," Max said. "We always need coaches." He winked at me. "We always need team captains too." Then he glided out of the room like he was on skates.

"Awesome," I whispered.

Chapter 3

On the way home from school, I gave my friends a talking-to.

"So we're all going to play hockey, right? It will be super fun, because we'll learn how to play together and we'll get to go to practices and games

together and we'll be together all the time, and it will be super fun." I said all of this with great fun-ness in my voice.

"Oh, Sylvie, I don't know," Miranda said. "I've got the science fair coming up, and I really need to spend every spare minute doing research. My project last year could have been so much better if I'd worked harder."

"You took first place in the district," I said.

She waved her hand at this, like first place meant nothing in the world of science. "If that had been a real science competition, the experiment would have been rejected because —"

"It's October," I said. "When is the science fair?"

"April," Miranda said.

"That's six months away, and I'll help you with your project." I put my hand over my heart. "Come on, you never do sports with me. Never."

Miranda's forehead went scrunchy. "That's because I don't like sports. Unless I'm watching you play."

I sighed, because convincing everyone was taking forever. "Hockey isn't a regular sport," I said. "Hockey is ice-skating with some other stuff, and you love to ice-skate, so you will love hockey!"

"I sort of like ice-skating," she said.

"But you also like math," I said, "and hockey is full of math! There are angles and triangles and squares and lines. The whole rink is an oval, and ice is probably a physical equation."

"Okay!" Miranda said. "Fine! I'll play hockey. But it's just for nine weeks, right?"

I smiled. I patted her on the shoulder. "It's just for nine weeks." I turned to Georgie.

"No," he said.

"You'll love it," I said. "It's like baseball, but with ice. And no bases."

Georgie had his no-way-am-I-listening-to-you face on. "It's not like baseball on ice," he said. "It's like soccer on ice, and I don't like soccer. Or ice."

My mouth fell open. How could someone not like ice?

"Hockey hurts," Georgie said. "It's the only sport where you run into walls."

"Not true," I said. "You run into walls in swimming. And golf."

"I saw a hockey player fall on his head once," Josh said. "But he had a helmet on, so he was probably okay. He only lost one tooth."

"I think they make pucks softer for kids," I said. "So you'll play?" I asked Georgie.

"No," he said.

Later that night, I tried to tell my mom and dad about hockey, but Tate and Cale had found a mountain of red ants right before dinner, and they needed an emergency bath.

I followed my dad into the bathroom and jumped up to sit on the counter. "I'm going to play hockey," I told him. "And Josh and Miranda and almost Georgie want to play too."

"That's great!" Dad said as he looked at his

watch. "Would you two get in the bath now? I'm in a hurry. Stop it, Cale, scratching will just make it worse."

"What's the oatmeal for?" Cale said with wide, scared eyes.

"For your bath," Dad said.

"Baths don't eat oatmeal," Tate said.

I stuck my head close to my dad to get his attention. "You could be my coach."

"The bath is not going to eat the oatmeal," Dad said to Tate. "It's supposed to soothe your ant bites. Don't you dare dump that in the toilet!"

There was a *plop* and a *splash*. Too late.

I waved my hands in front of my dad's face. "Max says they always need coaches. You could come to my practices. Like when you coached me in T-ball? Remember?"

"I wish I could," he said. "Where is that blasted plunger?"

"On the roof," Cale said.

"We're using it for antennas," Tate said, hopping in the bath.

"You'd be a fantastic coach," I told him. "The best in the whole league!"

"You two've been going on the roof again?" my dad said.

"Yes," Cale said, getting in the bath with his underwear on.

"No," Tate said.

"I might be team captain," I told my dad. "Max said."

My dad was trying to wrestle Cale out of the bathtub, but he paused to look at me. "I was captain of my hockey team." He smiled a great big smile. "You'd be a good team captain, sweetheart. I'd love to see that."

My mom stepped into the doorway with Ginny in her arms. "Sylvie," she said, her right eyebrow scrunched up at me, "I've asked you and asked you to clean up the bag of potato bugs you've got living in the hall."

"They're not living," I said. "They're dead. I'm storing them for Miranda." My dad was leaving the bathroom. "Where are you going?" I asked.

"Dinner with clients," my dad said. "I'll be back as soon as I can."

"But I might be in bed," I said, following him down the hallway. "And we need to talk about hockey."

"Later," he said. He opened the door to the garage like he was really going to go.

"Are you sure you don't want to coach?" I said.

"Bye!" he shouted as the door slammed.

"Bye," I whispered to the empty room.

Georgie found me in our classroom the next day. We had some time before the bell rang, so I was cleaning out Josh's cubby.

"Thanks a lot," Georgie said.

"You're welcome," I said as I threw away a paper airplane. There were lots of things that Georgie should thank me for, and I was glad he was now realizing this.

"Your mom called my house yesterday to see if my dad would coach the hockey team, and he said yes." Georgie did not look grateful. "Abuela made him. She told him we needed to spend more time together and since he played hockey in college, he should be my coach. Then she said I had to play too, because that nice Sylvie would be on my team." He didn't look like he thought I was a nice Sylvie. "What are you doing?" he said.

I moved some pencils over to the corner where I decided Josh should keep his pencils. "Josh is a disorganized person, so I am organizing him. Do you want me to organize you?" Georgie's cubby was famous for messiness. It overflowed with potato chip crumbs, baseball mitts, and suspicious-looking green clumps.

"Don't ever touch my stuff," Georgie said.

I gave him a very nice smile. "My dad wanted to be the coach," I said. "Only he couldn't because he's really busy with superimportant stuff. But I'm glad you finally decided to play. Our team will be awesome. We'll crush our opponents. We'll probably win the whole championship."

Georgie shrugged, picked a green clump out of his cubby, sniffed it, then ate it.

"We will," I said to reassure him. "I'm sure we'll win the whole thing."

Chapter 4

Two weeks later, my mom drove Miranda and me to our first practice.

"Don't be nervous," I told Miranda as we pulled into the parking lot. "It probably won't matter how good you are. Not with Georgie and me on the team. And I might be team captain."

"Sylvie," my mom said. "You keep talking about being team captain. Your dad wasn't team captain until he'd played hockey for a long time. There might be others on your team who are more qualified."

"Did you bring Band-Aids?" I asked Miranda.

"No," she said, sounding worried. "Do we need them?"

"Possibly," I said. "There could be bleeding. There's no pain, no gain in sports."

Miranda was quiet for a moment. "Is there any way to play sports without pain?"

"Yes," I said. "You can take ibuprofen whenever you need it. I brought an entire bottle of kids' chewable."

"Which you will now hand over to me," my mom said.

The skating rink was huge, probably the most ginormous skating rink ever, and it had a giant sign stretched across the ceiling that said ICE AIN'T NICE. It was full of coldness and echoes and sweaty sweat. Skates swished around the smooth frozen oval. Sticks hit pucks. People bashed into walls and into one another.

It was awesome.

"Oh!" Miranda cried. "It's cold. Really cold. I didn't think it would be this cold."

"It has to be cold if there's going to be ice," I explained patiently.

"Look," she said, holding her nose so it didn't freeze off. "There's Georgie's dad. And Georgie and Josh."

I looked out over the black rubber floor next to the ice. Georgie's dad stood in front of a bunch of kids in the bleachers. Bags of hockey stuff were everywhere. He held a clipboard in his hand and was calling out names.

"Hurry!" I said to Miranda, and we ran to the bleachers and sat down next to Josh.

"Alistair Robinson?" Georgie's dad was saying.

"Here!" said a boy in front of Josh. His voice sounded familiar, so I leaned sideways to get a look at him. It was that kid from Georgie's baseball team, the tiny one.

"Hi, Sylvie!" he said, turning around. "That's so cool you guys are on the team."

I looked at him sternly. He was so small. "Second graders aren't supposed to play hockey," I said. "It could be dangerous."

"I'm in third grade," he said.

"Sylvie Scruggs?" Georgie's dad said.

"I'm here!" I shouted. "And Miranda Tan's here too."

Georgie's dad looked up and I thought he smiled. It was hard to tell, because he was growing a mysterious beard. "Thank you, Sylvie. Good to see you. You too, Miranda. So that's it — oh, hang on! I missed somebody." He looked back down at his list. "Jamie Redmond — are you here?"

My pinky toes suddenly froze inside my wool socks. He could not have said that name.

"Here I am," Jamie Redmond said from behind me in her loud, horrible voice.

I turned around, and there she was. Jamie Redmond. Her arms were crossed, her head was tilted to the side, her eyes were half-shut, and her mouth wore a smirkity smirk. Her munions, the second baseman and the shortstop on her baseball team, sat on either side of her.

No, I thought. *No, no, no!!!!!!*

Georgie's dad began by explaining the hockey rules. Then he told us how to put on our uniforms, and he used Jamie as a model, because this was her fourth season playing hockey. We watched her put on her socks, her pants, her jersey, her shoulder pads, her elbow pads, her neck guard, her shin guards, her mouth guard, her helmet, her ice skates, and, okay, she was quick about it, but anyone can get dressed. Except for maybe babies and kings and queens.

When all this Jamie attention was through and we'd finished getting dressed ourselves, I raised my hand. "Who gets to be team captain?" I asked.

"The coach picks team captain," Coach Diaz said. "I will watch everyone throughout these first four practices. Whoever is the hardest working and the most helpful to his or her teammates will get the job. I'll announce team captain during the next to last practice before our first game."

Hardworking, I thought. *Helpful to teammates.* I could do that.

When we got out on the ice, Coach told us to skate around the oval so he could see how comfortable we were with our skates. "I want to see your feet in action," he said.

Our feet were pretty scary in action. Hardly anyone had skated before, and most of the team spent more time on their bottoms or their stomachs than on their feet. Ice-skating was easy for me, so I went around helping people up when they fell.

We were only supposed to be skating with our sticks, but partway through practice, Jamie Redmond dropped a puck on the ice and began pushing it toward the net. She moved slow and easy like a big, ugly swan. When she reached the net, she skidded to a stop, her stick high in the air. Then she swung it forward and hit the puck as hard as she could.

Swish. Score.

Miranda clapped. Georgie clapped. Josh clapped. The rest of the team clapped. Coach Diaz clapped. The people at the front desk clapped. If the president of the United States had been there, he would have clapped too.

"Wow," the tiny boy said to me with his mouth full of mouth guard. "Jamie's really good with the puck. Really, really good. And you're fat. Really, really fat. Probably the fattest."

"You think I'm fat?" I said.

"No!" He spit his mouth guard out inside his helmet. "I think you're fast, not fat!"

"Huh," I said.

The boy pulled off his helmet. "Do you want to come over to my house today? We could practice swinging our sticks."

"I can't," I told him. Coach wanted the team captain to be the hardest worker. I had to be a harder worker than Jamie Redmond. "I have to practice hockey," I said, "for reals."

"Time to try shooting!" Coach Diaz called.

"Oh, good!" I said, because this would be easy. If I could hit a baseball, I'd have no trouble hitting a puck. Pucks were flat! Way easier to hit than a round ball.

Everyone took a puck from Coach's bag except for Jamie Redmond. She was already in the center of the ice, moving one of her personal pucks around. Unlike Jamie, I am not a show-offy person, so I skated over to the side to try out my awesome hitting skills. My puck might fly far really fast, and I didn't want anyone to get hurt.

With the puck on the ice, I raised my stick. I took a deep breath of power. I closed my eyes.

Whoosh. That was the sound my stick made as it flew through the air.

Nothing. That was the sound my puck made as it stayed in the exact same place.

"Good effort, Sylvie!" Coach Diaz called in front of everybody. "But let's try that again!"

Jamie Redmond skated up and hit my puck into the net. *Swish.* "You have to watch the puck," she said with an evil smirk.

Coach hit another puck my way. I tried to stop it with my skate and fell over.

"That's okay," Josh said, helping me up.

"Man, our team's going to stink this year," one of Jamie's munions said to her in a whisper that was not really a whisper.

"It's all these little kids," Jamie said. "They're all third and fourth graders."

My face burned with anger. My bottom hurt from my fall. *I hate Jamie Redmond,* I thought. *And she hates me.* Over my aching body was she going to be team captain. No way.

I skated over to the bench and practically fell onto it from exhaustion. Miranda came over to join me. The skin on my cheeks felt dry, so I got out my special bottle of lotion that smelled like strawberries and rubbed some in. Then I picked up my water bottle, brought it to my mouth, and tilted my head back for a drink.

The lid popped off, hitting me smack in the face. Water gushed all over me.

"Oh!" I cried. "Oh no!" My face, my jersey, everything was sopping wet.

"Oh no!" Miranda echoed. "You're wet!"

"Quick!" I covered my soggy face with my hands. "Get me a towel."

Miranda handed me her towel. "Did you mean to do that?"

"No!" I shouted. Some of the others were looking. Josh. Jamie Redmond. That tiny boy, what's-his-name.

"You must have unscrewed the lid by accident," Miranda said.

I didn't argue, because I didn't want to discuss it out loud, but I knew she was wrong. I always screw my water bottle lids on tightly. Always.

Someone else must have loosened it.

Chapter 5

My dad came home late that night. I waited patiently while he played with Ginny. I waited patiently while he listened to the twins' knock-knock jokes, which were the same ones they told him yesterday. I waited patiently while my mom gave him a report on exactly how tired she was. I waited and waited and waited for him to ask me about practice.

Finally, I said, "I had hockey practice today."

"Oh!" my dad said. "That's right! I nearly forgot. How'd it go? I'm starving. Is that pot roast I smell?"

"Frozen burritos," Cale said.

Tate nodded. "But we're not allowed to say, 'Oh, man, again?'"

"Too true!" my dad said. "That's a rude thing to say, and frozen burritos never get old. Where's the salsa?"

"We're out," my mom said.

"Good!" my dad said. "Because I certainly don't want any."

"I was the fastest skater on the team," I said.

"Ginny only took two naps today," my mom said. "She's too young to be giving up her third."

"Who's there, Dad, who's there?" Tate said.

"You mean, knock, knock," Cale said.

"Underwear!" Tate said. Then he and Cale laughed so hard they knocked over their glasses of red punch.

"We only have three more practices until Coach Diaz picks team captain," I said while my dad mopped up the mess. "Just three."

"How was your math test today?" my mom asked me.

"Um, it happened," I said. I turned to the twins before my mom forced me to tell her more. "Isn't that a banana under there?"

"Underwear!" they both said, knocking over their glasses again.

35

"Dad?" I said later, after my mom and the twins and Ginny left to get ready for bed. He was staring at his cell phone while I cleared the table.

He rubbed his face, cursed modern technology, and jabbed the OFF button on his phone. "Yes, honey?" he said.

He was looking at me now, which made me forget what I wanted to say.

"Did you have a question?" he said.

"Yes!" I said. "I did. I mean, do. I do have a question. It's about team captains. What is the most important thing to do if you want to be team captain? Be a good skater, or be a good shooter?"

My dad rubbed his face again, but he didn't get up or turn on his cell phone. "Both are equally important," he said. "But what really matters is how you unify the team. Build up the other players."

"What do you mean?" I said.

"Compliment your teammates when they do well," he said. "Steer clear of fighting. You have to be the one everyone looks up to as a model of good behavior."

My face scrunched up. Wow. A model of good behavior. That would be hard.

"Our next practice is this Friday," I said. "After school. You could come watch."

"Oh, I'd like to, sweetheart, but I've got a meeting. I'll be at your first game for sure."

Mom called him then to help put the boys down once and for all and forever. He rubbed his hand over his face one more time and left.

I finished clearing the table and stuck the dishes in the dishwasher. Then, with three chocolate-chip cookies in my pocket, I went to the bathroom, turned on the fan, and shut the door. I climbed up next to the sink and stared at my freckly face. Jamie Redmond would not be good at uniting the team. I could skate and she could shoot, but the one who united the team would probably win.

"Good job, Carolina!" I said into the mirror, thinking of the girl on my team who hadn't let go of the wall during practice. "Way not to cry too hard when you fall down. Yo, Michael!" I said. "Nice swing. I like the way you bend that elbow. Way to go, Ravi! Don't let anyone tell you you're too tall. Good job, Josh. That was great how you stopped going the wrong way."

I smiled in the mirror, letting my teeth show. Then I stopped.

I'd have to be careful not to smile like that while I unified people. It was a little scary.

At Friday's practice, Coach gathered us around before we got on the ice. "I want everyone to start thinking of names for our team. We'll vote on a team name before our first game, which is just four practices away now."

A team name! *What would make a good hockey team name?* I wondered. The Killers, maybe? The Pouncers? The Ice Cheetahs?

Then practice began. "Good job, Miranda!" I called as she skated up to me. "Ooo, that was quick!" I said to Michael as he went past. "Really, really quick. Love the way you bend your knees, Tamara. It makes a nice angle. Nice job, Georgie. Way to, um, glide."

Georgie looked like he wished I would glide all the way to Africa. Unifying him was going to be hard.

"I like your attitude, Sylvie!" Coach Diaz called to me.

I smiled without showing my teeth.

"Watch this, Sylvie!" that small kid said, the one from Georgie's baseball team. He turned around and skated away so fast, he didn't see the three biggest kids on our team standing in his way. He looked like a runaway bowling ball heading toward three gigantic pins. They knocked him over instead of the other way around.

Puck practice came next. The first time I tried to shoot, I missed. The second time I tried to shoot, I missed. The third time I tried to shoot, I accidentally let go of my stick and it flew halfway across the rink.

The fourth time I missed, I fell onto my back and stayed there for a very long time.

"Sylvie," Coach said, "you look like you're giving up. You're not, are you?"

"No, Coach," I said, still not moving because I couldn't remember how. *What is the matter with me?*

I wondered. How could someone who is so good at pitching stink so much at hitting a tiny little puck?

"Hey, Georgie!" the tiny boy said as he skated by again.

"Hey, Alistair," Georgie said.

"Don't encourage him," I whispered to Georgie. "Alisonair's too little to play. He's going to get hurt."

"His name is Alistair," Georgie said.

I nodded. "And he's way too small."

The boy was standing beside us all of a sudden. "Are you talking about me?"

"We were talking about smallness," I said. Then I patted him on the shoulder pad to make him feel better.

"Break!" Coach Diaz called, and everyone took off for the benches.

Before I sat down on the bench, I checked my water-bottle lid for tightness. It was as tight as a tiger's jaw, so I took a drink, then got out my special strawberry lotion. *You will not give up*, I chanted to myself as I popped open the lid. *You will work harder than anyone else!* I took a deep breath, expecting to smell strawberries. I couldn't smell them. *You will unify everyone,* I thought as I shook the bottle hard. The lotion wasn't coming out. *Jamie will never be team captain.* At last, out plopped a blob. *And Dad will come to all my games.*

I put some lotion on my arm. Then I sniffed. Definitely not strawberries.

"Why does it stink in here?" Georgie said.

That tiny boy — I think Georgie called him Avatar — sat down next to me on the bench. He looked at my arm. He sniffed.

Miranda has especially good nostrils because she's a scientist. "It smells like mayonnaise," she said.

I looked down at my hand. The lotion was extra-blobby and extra-slimy. It wouldn't rub in. I sniffed again. "Ugh!" I cried. "It is mayonnaise!"

"You put mayonnaise on your arm?" one of Jamie's munions said. "Nasty!"

"Mega-gross," the other one said.

"Maybe she's saving it as a snack for later," Jamie said.

Oh boy, the munions thought that was funny.

"Go to the bathroom and clean it off," Miranda whispered. I got up and hurried to the bathroom with my lotion bottle in my hand. Everyone laughed as I fled.

Inside the bathroom, I locked my stall door and stood over the toilet. I squeezed the rest of the white gloopy stuff into the toilet bowl. Was it really mayonnaise? Or had something happened to my lotion? How could mayonnaise get into my strawberry lotion bottle?

Coach Diaz was setting up a demonstration when I returned to the ice. "Oh, there you are," he said to me. "I want you and Jamie to show us what it will look like when you're racing down the ice with an opponent on your tail. Jamie will have the puck" — the munions grinned — "and Sylvie will follow, showing us how to block her."

I looked at Miranda. She gave me a smile and a thumbs-up and a "You can do this, Sylvie!" look. I skated over to Coach. I nodded my head. I tried not to think about mayonnaise.

Coach blew his whistle. He slid a puck toward us. Jamie caught it with her stick and took off for the net.

Go! I told myself. *Go get her!* So I did. I shot off like a cheetah, my skates sliding down the ice. I caught up to Jamie in no time, then pushed myself

ahead of her so she had to dodge out of my way. I forced her to the right; I forced her to the left.

"Go away," she said with a snarl. "You're going to knock me over, mayonnaise girl!"

But I didn't go away, and she didn't score. Not until she tripped me with her stick. After that, she scored.

"Good shot, Jamie!" Coach said. "Good defense, Sylvie!"

"She tripped me with her stick!" I said. "Isn't that against hockey rules?"

But Coach was already putting everyone else in pairs to practice. "Jamie and Sylvie, switch positions!" he shouted. Then he blew his whistle.

Jamie dropped a puck on the ice. "You should pay more attention," she said.

Pay attention — I always paid attention! I swung my stick and paid attention. The puck went flying up into the air. *Hooray!* I thought. *I did it!*

"Ow!" that boy — Armino, I think — cried as the puck flew into his leg.

"Are you all right — ow!" I shouted, because Jamie had smacked me in the back of the leg with her stick. A puck was coming our way. Jamie shoved me with her hip and stole it. Then she skated down the ice and scored. Again.

"Nice work, Jamie!" Coach said.

When practice ended, I stomped off the ice. This had been a horrible practice. I hadn't scored one goal, and it was all Jamie's fault. She distracted me with her smirks and her laughs and her advice.

I took off my skates and zipped up my bag. Well, there'd be no more of that. Jamie would never get the bester part of me again. I would figure out how to hit that puck before next practice, or my name wasn't Sylvie Elizabeth Scruggs the First.

I was about to stand up when I saw something hiding next to my bag. It was a small glass jar. I bent over to pick it up, but stopped when I saw the label.

MAYONNAISE, it said in bright blue letters.

The jar was mostly empty, but there were white globby smears on both the inside and outside. A tiny piece of paper sat on the lid. Careful not to touch the mayonnaise, I picked it up and opened it.

Chapter 6

I thought about that Gotcha note all night (except for when I was sleeping). Someone had put mayonnaise in my lotion bottle on purpose, and whoever it was had probably unscrewed the lid to my water bottle too.

Someone was out to get me.

But who? Whoever left that note couldn't be on my team, because they were practicing while I was practicing, and I didn't know anyone else in the hockey rink. Why would a stranger prank me unless they had some sort of pranking disease?

At seven o'clock a.m. time, I called Miranda. "We need to practice hockey," I said. "And we need to figure out who is pranking me."

"Sylvie?" Miranda said. "Is this you?" She

sounded like she hadn't planned on me calling this early in the morning.

"We have to meet," I said, "any minute now. Will you call Georgie?"

"Sure," she said after a giant yawn. "But why don't you call him?"

"Because he's a boy," I said.

"But I'm a girl and I call Georgie."

"You're a scientist," I said. "That's different."

"But you call Josh."

"Briskly," I said. "I call Josh briskly. Be here by nine o'clock a.m. time. My dad's making waffles."

"Will the twins be there?" she said. The last time Miranda came over, the twins put slugs in her hair.

"Yes," I said. "But it's all right. My mom made them put their slug collection outside."

"Oh!" she said with relief. "Good."

"Call Georgie now, okay?"

"Roger," Miranda said.

"No," I said. "Don't call Roger, I don't even know who Roger is. Call Georgie."

Then I called Josh.

"Hello," I said. "It's me."

"I know," Josh said.

I paused. "What do you mean, you know?"

"I mean, I know it's you."

"But who do you think 'you' is?" I said. "I haven't told you yet."

"It's always you," Josh said.

"What do you mean, 'It's always you'?"

"I mean, whenever anyone calls me and they say, 'It's me,' it's always you."

"What?" I said.

"Huh?" he said.

"Let's stop talking about it," I said sharply. "Be at my house at nine o'clock a.m. time. There will be waffles."

"Okay," Josh said. "I'll see you. You, you, I mean."

At nine o'clock sharp a.m. time, Josh rang the doorbell.

I opened the door. "Come in," I said, and Josh came in.

"Nice day for waffles," I said, because someone had to say something.

"I like waffles," Josh said.

"Tate!" my dad shouted from inside the kitchen. "Stop dropping dental floss in the waffle batter. It won't make them minty!"

Josh glanced in the direction of the kitchen. He bit his lip.

The doorbell rang again. It was Miranda and Georgie. I showed them into the dining room, and we sat down at the table. "We have to eat fast," I told them. "We don't have much time to practice. Just all day today and all day tomorrow. We can't practice Monday because we have to go to school."

"Cale!" my dad shouted. "Not cat food!"

"Did you get a cat?" Miranda said.

"I don't think so," I said.

Georgie was looking stubborn — his pretty-much-normal look. "I don't want to practice hockey," he said. "I came here for waffles."

"We have to practice," I informed him. "We stink."

"You mean you stink," he said.

"You stink worse," I said.

Georgie nodded, but said, "You just want to beat Jamie Redmond."

"I do not!" I pounded my fist on the table. "Come on, we're wasting time. We also need to figure out who put the mayonnaise in my lotion bottle."

"Oh, that's easy," Georgie said, leaning back in his seat and crossing his arms. "It was Jamie."

A stunned silence hit the table. "What did you say?" I said into the stunning silence.

Tate entered the dining room wearing a flowered apron on his head. "I am now presenting the first waffle." He set a plate in front of Georgie. He let out an omnivorous giggle. "Enjoy."

Georgie ignored the giggle and dove right in. He

chewed for a few seconds, then spat out a yellow LEGO piece.

"You saw Jamie put mayonnaise in my lotion?" I said.

Georgie rinsed off the LEGO in his orange juice. "I saw her zipping up your bag during practice."

Cale came in the dining room with a waffle for Josh.

"Is that a piece of paper?" Josh said, pointing to something sticking out from the side of the waffle.

"It's a check," Cale said. "I took it from my dad's wallet. In case you need money."

Josh pulled the check out slowly. It was covered in waffle chunks.

"When did you see her?" I said to Georgie.

"I don't know. Sometime during practice."

"During practice! What was she doing exactly?"

Georgie put his palm against his forehead like I was wearing him out. "She was pulling on the zipper. Shutting it. I think."

"You think? Did she put something in my bag first?"

"I don't know," he said again. "Alistair was blocking my view."

"I think we should be nicer to Alistair," Miranda said. "He seems lonely."

"I'm not hungry anymore," Georgie said, looking at something hairy he'd just found in his waffle. Probably cat food.

"I'm not hungry either," Josh said, standing up. "Let's go practice."

Miranda practically ran out the back door after them.

I stayed at the table. Jamie Redmond put the mayonnaise in my lotion bottle. It made perfect sense. She wanted to be team captain, and she was afraid Coach might choose me. I was her competition. I was her enemy.

"You should get her back," Georgie said, many hours later. We were in my backyard. We'd been hitting bouncy balls with our hockey sticks all morning. My arms were tired. Miranda looked saggy. Josh kept yawning.

"We don't know it was Jamie," Miranda said for the bazillionth time.

"Maybe you should try to get proof," Josh said.

"How do I do that?" I asked.

"Catch her the next time she tries to prank you."

"I can't," I said. "She pranks me during practice, and I have to play hockey. I can't just stare at my bag."

"You could bring the twins," Georgie said. "They could guard your stuff."

"No," Miranda said. "That's a terrible idea.

They're too little — Sylvie would have to watch them the whole time."

It was an intriguing idea, even though it came from Georgie. "If I paid them, they might be good," I said.

"They don't care about money," Miranda said, meaning "Please, Sylvie, think. Don't do this."

"I have jelly beans," I said. "They love jelly beans."

Georgie nodded because jelly beans are good. "Let's take a vote," he said.

"Okay," Miranda said. "All who think Sylvie should pretend nothing happened, say, 'Aye, aye!'" Then she said, "Aye, aye!" with a terrible pirate accent.

Georgie smiled without showing his teeth. "All who think Sylvie should bring the twins to the rink to catch Jamie in the act of pranking, say, 'Aye, aye!'"

"Aye, aye!" Josh and Georgie said.

"Aye, aye," I said, without looking at Miranda, who was probably thinking about slugs.

Chapter 7

On Monday after school, a miracle happened. My mom needed to take Ginny to a doctor's appointment and my dad had a work meeting, so he called our neighbor Gloria Zhu to babysit. Gloria told my dad she thought it would be fun to bring the twins to my practice, and my dad actually believed her. What Gloria didn't tell my dad was that she had a crush on Peter Sullivan, who worked at the arcade inside the skating rink.

"I'm just going to step into the arcade," Gloria said when we got to the benches next to the ice. "Do you think you two can be good and stay here and watch Sylvie's practice?"

"Oh yes," Cale said. "We are always good. Especially when we sit."

"You don't need to watch us at all," Tate said. "You can stay in the arcade the whole time."

"I'll keep an eye on them," I told her, because I needed her to go away.

Gloria darted off like a lovesick hyena.

I'd already explained the Jamie situation to my brothers. They knew exactly what to do.

"So we're supposed to watch a guy named James and see if he does anything to your bottles?" Tate said.

"No," Cale said. "We're supposed to be quiet and watch a girl named Jamie in case she throws something at Sylvie's bag. And we can't talk. Not ever. Not even to burp. And we're not supposed to tell Jamie that we're watching her."

"Can we tell her if she has a zit?" Tate said.

"Just sit still and watch my bag," I said through gritty teeth.

"Okay!" Tate and Cale said. They looked down at my bag and opened their eyes wide.

I sighed because I always sigh about my brothers and skated onto the ice. It was time to unify. "Are you ready for a great practice, Ravi?" I said. "Quinn, I love that sticker on your hockey bag. 'Barf bag,' that's funny. Hey, Jamie's munion — I mean, friend — I like your braid! Oh, sorry. I won't talk to you anymore."

Coach Diaz blew his whistle, and we gathered around him on the ice. "Okay, folks, we've only got three practices left before our first game. I'm going to be on the lookout for a team captain today, so work your hardest. We're going to split into two groups and run some drills. Josh, do you remember where I put that list?"

While Josh helped Coach find his list, Jamie announced that she had selected the perfect name for our team. "The Rockets," she said.

One side of my nose went up higher than the other. The Rockets? Talk about a snoozefest.

"What about the Ice Cheetahs?" I said, whipping out my best name.

"The Ice Cheetahs?" Jamie said, like I'd said, "The Skunk Bottoms."

"I like the Ice Cheetahs," the tiny boy said, Apollo or whatever his name was. "Or maybe the Ice Serpents. Or the Sabertooths!"

"No," I said. "Those are third-grade names."

"The Sabertooths isn't bad," Jamie said.

"We don't want to be named after an extinct animal," I said. "That would mean we died."

Coach blew his whistle. "Pick a side!" he shouted.

I glanced toward the benches, where I expected

to see my brothers sitting quietly. Cale was sitting quietly. Tate was not. He was nowhere in sight.

"Where's Tate?" I mouthed at Cale.

"I'm not allowed to talk!" he shouted. Then he covered his eyes and said, "Oops."

"Sylvie!" Coach Diaz called. "Everyone's in position but you."

I got into position, then checked the bench. Tate was still missing.

"I call this drill 'Eat the Puck,'" Coach said. "Each of you will get a puck. Then you'll skate toward the opposite goal, keeping the puck inside your stick. If you make it to the blue line in front of the net without losing your puck, you may shoot, but if you lose the puck, you have to start over." Coach said it was a skating drill and a puck-handling drill mixed into one. Only the truly focused would survive.

I looked at the benches. Now Cale was gone too. How was I supposed to focus when my brothers had disappeared?

Coach set pucks in front of everyone. He blew his whistle. The rest of my team began taking their pucks down the ice. My brothers weren't by the benches. They weren't in the lobby.

Coach blew his whistle again, long and loud.

"All right, we're running that one more time. Sylvie, you didn't even move."

"Oh," I said. "Sorry! I, um, forgot." I looked at Miranda. "Have you seen my brothers?" I mouthed. Miranda's eyes got big.

The whistle blew. Then it blew again.

"Sylvie!" Coach called. "When I blow the whistle, you have to go. Michael nearly ran you over."

"Okay!" I called. "Sorry, Coach."

Forget about the twins! I told myself. *What's the worst that could happen?*

I really hoped they hadn't brought matches.

The whistle blew. I focused on the puck. It was in my stick. I skated forward and — hooray! — it was still there. I approached the goal. My heart pounded.

My head thumped. I was going to do it. I was actually going to score. I lifted my stick.

Buzzzzzzzzzzzzzz!

I dropped my stick. The buzzing sound kept going.

"What's that noise?" a munion shouted.

"It's hurting my ears!" Michael called.

"Look at that kid!" Jamie Redmond yelled.

She was pointing at the drink machine over by the concession stand. There was Tate, standing beneath the drink spout, his head tilted back, his mouth open. Cale was punching the button that makes the soda come out. Orange soda poured from the machine straight into Tate. The machine was making the buzzing sound. It didn't like being punched.

"Hey!" the rink manager shouted. "What are you doing to my drink machine?"

"It won't turn off!" Cale cried, punching the button faster and harder.

Glug, glug, glug! went Tate.

"Get away!" the rink manager hollered.

Tate stopped guzzling. Cale stopped punching the button, but the soda kept flowing. My brothers ran over to the bench, sat down, wiped their orange-covered faces with their hands, and smiled. Except for Tate. He burped before he smiled.

"It's jammed!" the rink manager cried. Three moms ran over and fixed the machine. I was glad they did. Watching that soda was making me have to go to the bathroom.

Coach ran a hand through his hair until it stood straight up from his head. "Show's over, kids. Let's run that drill again."

He blew his whistle. I glared at Tate and Cale and pointed at the bench. "Stay!" I mouthed furiously. Then I began to skate down to the opposite net with my puck. I raced faster, and the puck moved faster as well. I was nearly at the net now, and I was going to score!

Jamie Redmond slid up next to me. Her stick went up in the air. I raised mine too.

A puck flew by us, straight into the net. Jamie and I dropped our arms and turned around. Josh was standing behind us, looking surprised.

"Ha!" the tiny boy shouted. "That was awesome. Josh beat both of you!"

"Great shot, Josh!" Coach Diaz called. He blew his whistle. "Run it again!"

"Where did you come from?" I said to Josh.

"Down there," Josh said, pointing to the other side of the rink.

"Ahhhhhhhhhhhh!"

I knew that scream. It was a five-year-old-twin-boy scream. I looked over at the benches. My brothers were gone again.

"Ahhhhhhhhhhhh!"

I could see them now. They had hockey sticks in their hands and they were chasing each other around the rink. The rink manager was chasing them too.

"Sylvie," Coach Diaz said. "Maybe you'd better take care of that."

"Yes, Coach," I said.

It took forever to catch my brothers. Then I had to listen to a lecture from the rink manager and a lecture from Gloria, who was mad that she had to leave the arcade.

It was a serious march back to the bench.

"I'm going on the ice," I whispered to my brothers with the firmness of a tiger. "Keep an eye on my bag."

"Keeping an eye on your bag would hurt," Cale said.

"Unless her bag was made of water," Tate said.

Coach Diaz blew his whistle. "Practice time is up!"

My mouth fell open. "Practice is over? It can't be over! It practically just started."

"It is over," Gloria said. "It's four thirty, and I have to go to the bathroom really fast. Watch your brothers for me." Then she walked off toward the arcade, not the bathroom.

But I really did have to go to the bathroom. It was almost an emergency. "Wait —" I shouted after Gloria. "I have to go to the bathroom too!"

"I could watch the twins for you," the tiny boy, Archimedes or something, said. "But I think the regular bathroom is full. You should use the secret bathroom."

"The secret bathroom?" I said.

"It's the bathroom the coaches and the rink manager use. It's down that hall, back by the janitor's closet. My brother told me about it."

A line was forming outside the girls' bathroom. There was no way I'd last that long. "Thanks," I said to Archimedes. Then I snuck down the hallway past the regular bathrooms until I came to the janitor's closet, full of brooms and vacuums. The secret bathroom was right beside it. I flipped on the light and tiptoed inside.

The room was tiny with just one toilet and one sink. I took care of business and was just about to wash my hands when a piece of paper slid beneath the door. *Weird,* I thought.

A vacuum sound turned on. A cloud of white blew up into the bathroom. It blew onto the walls and the floor. It blew up on my hair and skin and all over my clothes. I covered my face with my hands as the white stuff got into my eyes and mouth.

I'm being attacked by dust! I thought. But this wasn't dust. Dust would be dustier, and it would smell bad. This stuff smelled good, like Ginny when my mom changed her diaper. Baby powder!

The vacuum sound ended and I put my hands down. White stuff still floated in the air, but most of it had settled. The bathroom was a mess. My entire body was covered in baby powder. I looked like a Sylvie ghost.

Footsteps came down the hallway. I had to clean this mess up fast. The baby powder wouldn't brush off, so I turned a knob on the sink. Water exploded from the faucet, shooting up into the air. I screamed and tried to turn it off, but the knob broke off in my hand. I backed away, only then noticing the OUT OF ORDER sign below the mirror.

There was a pounding on the door. "Hey! What's going on in there?"

Oh no! It was the rink manager. Maybe I could jam up the sink so the water would stop. I ran to the paper towel holder, but none of the towels were poking out.

"Open up!" he growled.

"Just a minute," I said. I pushed my hand up into the paper towel holder to get the towels, but my fingers got stuck. "Ow!" I whispered. "Ow, ow, ow!"

I heard the jangle of keys.

"Hold on!" I shrieked as I tried to pull my hand out.

The door opened. The rink manager looked at me. He looked at the bathroom. "What is this? No one's supposed to touch that sink!"

While the manager rushed toward the fountain of water, Coach Diaz walked into the bathroom. Half the team was behind him. "Oh my goodness!" he said. "Sylvie, are you stuck?"

"Look at her!" Jamie Redmond said as she and her munions peered in the doorway. "She's covered in baby powder, and she broke the bathroom!"

"Ha ha ha ha ha ha!" everybody said.

Chapter 8

My dad came to my room later that night to tuck me in. I kicked my blankets around so they were messy and tucking me in would take a long, long time. I made my face calm so he'd want to stay.

"How's my little team captain?" he said.

Team captain. My heart shrunk in my chest. I hadn't scored today. I hadn't even done a good job unifying. The rink manager had yelled a lecture at me until Georgie's dad told him I didn't break the bathroom on purpose.

"What's the matter?" my dad said.

"Nothing," I said quickly. "Did I tell you that I'm the fastest on my team?"

"Doesn't surprise me," he said, leaning on the bed with one elbow. "How do you handle the puck?"

"I almost scored today," I said.

"Almost?" my dad said.

"It was close." I picked at an orange thread on my quilt. It was a loose thread. If I pulled hard enough, it would come right out.

"I wasn't good at shooting when I first started playing," my dad said.

"Really?" I pushed at the orange thread so it would go into place.

"You should see if you can get some special help with your shooting."

"Could you help me?" I asked. "You'd be great at special help."

My dad sat up. "I wish I had time, but I'm so busy right now. Maybe later in the season."

Which meant no. I stopped pushing the loose thread. "Dad?" I said. "What do you do if you think someone is trying to get you?"

"'Get you'?" he said. "What do you mean, 'get you'?"

"Like they want to play pranks on you," I said.

"Pranks?"

I looked down at the thread. "Like maybe they loosened the lid on your water bottle so water pours all over your face. That kind of thing."

"Is this happening to you?" my dad said. He sounded disappointed. No one wanted a kid who got water bottles dumped on their face.

"I'm speaking metaphysically," I said.

"Metaphysically, huh?" He sighed. "Well, I'd probably start by standing up for myself."

That was a grown-up kind of answer that wasn't any use. "You mean getting them back?" I said. "Like revenge?"

A crash came from somewhere down the hall. "Sam!" my mom shouted. "Help! Cale's stuck in the bathroom cupboard again!"

"Sort of," my dad said, leaping to his feet. He aimed a kiss at my forehead but missed. "Good night, sweetheart."

He flipped off the light and ran from the room. I watched him go, then pounded a fist on the orange thread. I needed to get revenge on Jamie Redmond, plus I needed to find special help. But how was I supposed to do that?

"Do you know a boy named Max?" I asked my brothers the next morning. Tate and Cale know everyone in the neighborhood, and everyone in the neighborhood knows them. "He's a high school boy," I said. "And a champion hockey player. He might live around here." Max was the only person I could think of who could give me special help besides my dad.

"We know him," Tate said. "We call him Mad Max."

Cale nodded. "And his sisters are Madder Hattie and Maddest Tess."

"They're twin girls our age, and we hate them," Tate said. "They have another brother too — I forget his name."

"We went to their house once," Cale said. "Mom thought it would be a good idea for twins to be friends with other twins, even though they're girl twins."

"It wasn't a good idea," Tate said. "Except we got to taste Mad Max's secret hockey training juice. He wants to sell it for a million dollars."

"It tastes like cotton candy smashed into water," Cale said.

"It was epic," Tate said. "He lives way down on Josh's street."

Secret hockey training juice? That sounded interesting. "Will you take me there if I pick you up from kindergarten today?"

"No," Tate said.

"Yes," Cale said.

"Good," I said, hurrying off to tell my mom to write their teacher a note. I don't normally pick them up from school because it's like herding wild hyenas, but today would have to be an exemption.

Team captains shouldn't need special help, so I told Miranda and Josh and Georgie that my mom was making me pick up the twins from school. "You guys had better walk home without me," I said. "It's going to take a long time, because the twins refuse to walk. They skip the whole way home. And they insist on starting over if they skip on a crack."

"There are a lot of cracks in the sidewalk," Josh said.

"Exactly," I said. "You shouldn't have to suffer with me."

So my friends left, and I picked up my brothers alone, no problem. We saw no one important as we walked out of the school and into our neighborhood. No one would ever know where we were going. No one would know I needed special help.

We were walking up to Max's house when my friends appeared. Just like that. "We were waiting for you at your house, but you never came," Miranda said.

"This is the house of that hockey player," Josh said. "The one that came to our class."

"What are you doing here?" Georgie said.

Shoot, shoot, shoot! I thought. I tried to look boring so they would go home. "The twins are friends with his little sisters," I explained.

"No, we're not," Tate said.

"We hate them," Cale said. "They are not epic."

I sighed, imagining a panther covering my

brothers' mouths with its paws so they could never speak again.

"We'll come with you," Josh said.

"Oh, that's okay," I said, but Georgie was already following my brothers up to the porch. Miranda, Josh, and I ran after them. The front door flew open. In the doorway were two twin girls with matching outfits and matching scowls.

"We are ghosts," Tate said, raising his arms up like a ghost. "And we hate you!"

"Yeah," Cale said, trying to cross his arms but getting confused. "Woooooooooo!"

"We hate you too," one girl said. "Want to play with the lab rats?"

"Yes!" my brothers said, and they all dashed inside the house.

The rest of us were left at the open front door.

"That was weird," Georgie said.

"Hey!" a voice shouted from above.

We backed up until we could see the person hanging out the window. It was Max.

"Who are you?" he said.

I didn't know what to say. I couldn't say Sylvie Scruggs. Sylvie Scruggs was nobody. "We're hockey players!" I shouted.

"Excellent!" Max cried. "Come on up. I'm in the middle of an energy drink experiment." His head disappeared.

"Well, I guess I'll go in," I said in my boringest voice. "You guys can go home now."

"I want to see an experiment," Miranda said.

"I want to try an energy drink," Georgie said.

"I don't think any of us should go in there," Josh said.

Miranda walked past me and straight up the stairs like she knew exactly where to go. Georgie, Josh, and I caught up to her in the upstairs hallway. Someone had written Max's Laboratory in glitter pen on a white door.

The door opened and Max stood to the side, waving us in. We entered a room stuffed with scientific things: inventions made with crepe paper and elastics and tinfoil, sculptures made with gears and pipes and tissue paper, a neon-green micro-scope, and beakers full of colorful liquids, bubbling gently.

In the center of the small room was a table, and in the center of the table was a glass bottle filled with red liquid. Right next to the bottle was a fat white rat with bright pink eyes sitting in a glass tank. It turned its head to look at us. Then it ran straight forward, bonking its nose on the glass. It kept running around in circles while Max whipped out a stopwatch.

"Excellent," he said. "It took two minutes for the energy juice to take effect."

"What are the drink's primary ingredients?" Miranda asked in her scientific-est voice.

"Mostly sugar," Max said. Then he launched into a description of his plan to sell the juice for a million dollars. "It will give athletes extra strength," he said. "So their bodies will do what they're supposed to do."

I stared at that glass bottle with the red liquid. That's exactly what I needed. A drink to tell my arms and hands how to hit the puck. "Can I have some?" I said, reaching out to touch the bottle.

Max pulled it away. "Sorry," he said.

"Not even a taste?" Georgie said. Georgie really likes sugar.

But Max was firm. "It's not ready yet. There might be side effects. I have to do some human trials."

"Which would be totally inappropriate on children," Miranda said.

"Exactly," Max said. "Unless they are related to you. Now, I'm assuming you're here for hockey advice?"

I gasped in wonder. "How did you know?"

He shrugged like it was no big deal. "That's the only advice I give. People usually don't want to know about science, and I'm no good at relationship questions."

"Relationship questions?" Georgie said in absolute disgust.

"I can't get the puck into the net," I said.

"She can't hit the puck at all," Georgie said.

I put my fists on my hips. "That's not true. I can hit the puck. Just not when I want to."

"Interesting," Max said. "Hitting the puck takes lots of practice, and I can't help you with that, because it's something you just have to do. But I will tell you the secret that helps me no matter what I'm struggling with."

I held my breath and nodded. A secret!

"You should pretend you are a torpedo," Max said.

I let out my breath. "A torpedo?" I said.

"A torpedo?" Georgie repeated, like that was the stupidest thing he'd ever heard.

Max nodded as if he'd expected doubt. "A torpedo is a really fast bomb that zooms through water to blow up other ships. It's made of steel and it's practically unstoppable. You've got to tell yourself that you are made of steel, just like a torpedo. That you are unstoppable. That even the ice is afraid of you."

"The ice should be afraid of us?" Josh said.

"Oh yes," Max said. "The ice should be very afraid of you. That's what you need to remember. You are the dangerous thing. You are the awesomeness. You may want to meditate about that — you are the awesomeness."

"I am the awesomeness," I whispered. No one — not even Jamie — could stop me.

But it would help if I had some secret power juice.

"Where'd the brown one go?" Cale shouted from somewhere down the hall.

"I see a tail," Tate cried. "Rats are even faster than ferrets. This is epic!"

"At last!" a girl yelled. "They're free!"

"Not again!" Max shouted. Then he darted from the room.

"We'd better get out of here," Josh said. "Come on, Sylvie."

"I'm coming," I said, taking one last look at Max's special drink, so red and so powerful. I'd do anything to get some of that juice.

Just be a torpedo, I told myself. *Be a torpedo, and nothing will stop you.*

Chapter 9

I was the busiest person in the universe on Wednesday and Thursday. I had to practice unifying the team in the mirror. I had to practice being a torpedo in my backyard with my stick and my bouncy balls. And I had to think up revenge on Jamie for the pranks.

By the time Friday afternoon rolled around, I was ready. I was going to prove to Coach Diaz at this practice — the last practice before he would announce team captain — that I was his number-one hockey player.

When I got to the rink, I walked straight to the benches where I found Alvinair, or whatever his name was, sitting, swinging his legs.

He jumped to his feet when he saw me. "I didn't do anything!" he said.

I frowned with my eyebrows. "Good," I said. "You should probably never do things. Now, I am going to meditate, so please don't speak to me."

His eyes widened as if he'd never heard of anyone meditating before a hockey practice. I knew all about meditating because Miranda's mom used to have a boyfriend who meditated and we spied on him once. I sat on the ground, legs crossed, hands resting palms-up on my knees. I closed my eyes. "This is how you meditate," I told him. "Fourth graders do it all the time. No talking."

I began to lightly hum. I thought about torpedoes. I imagined a purple torpedo with my face at one end. I imagined the torpedo had arms, and it held a hockey stick in its hands. It sailed around with the puck in its stick, knocking over faceless opponents. Okay, maybe one player had a face and okay, maybe she was on my team. And okay, maybe her name was Jamie.

Then my purple torpedo-self hit the puck into the net with one perfect swing. I imagined this ten times. Then I pictured my whole team as a rainbow of torpedoes. Okay, except for Jamie. We floated around the rink until we became one giant torpedo ring, which was perfect because rings are unified and they remind me of doughnuts. I pictured my torpedo-self eating a chocolate doughnut with sprinkles. Then I pictured my torpedo-self hitting a chocolate doughnut with sprinkles into the net. Then I ate that too. (The doughnut, not the net.)

Alvinair tapped me on the shoulder. "I brought this for you," he said.

I opened my eyes. "Where did you get that?" I whispered. It was Max's bottle of secret juice.

"Just someplace," he said. "It will help you score for sure. You'd better drink it fast."

He was right. Miranda or Georgie or Josh might try to stop me.

I grabbed the bottle and pulled out the cork. Eyes closed, I took one big gulp. My mouth burned as the sugary redness slunk down my throat. I rubbed at my neck. It hurt to swallow. I needed something to wash it down, so I drank some more. I finished the entire bottle.

A headache burst into my forehead. My throat felt like a panther was scratching it with its claws.

I grabbed my water bottle, checked the lid before opening it, and gulped down the whole thing.

When I was done, I dropped the bottle and clutched my stomach with both hands. An angry whirlpool of red juice and water churned inside of me, trying to find a way out.

Just wait, I told myself. *In minutes, you will feel powerful. You will feel like a torpedo.*

The whistle blew and everyone skated onto the

ice. I moved woozily behind them, the liquid slosh-ing around in my belly. "Do you feel like a torpedo?" I asked Michael, trying to unify him.

He looked at me like I was a panther and skated away.

Coach began talking about puck work. He talked and talked until his words spun around, making me dizzy. My skin felt strange, and my lips tingled. I raised my hand.

"Sylvie?" Coach said. "Sylvie? Are you all right?"

Everyone turned to look at me.

"Oh no," Josh said.

Miranda gasped. "You look like you're going to faint!"

"What's that red stuff on your face?" Jamie Redmond said.

"It's lipstick," one of her munions said, laughing historically.

My stomach lurched. A wave of coldness hit me like an ocean plunging over my head.

"She looks green," Georgie said.

"Oh no!" Jamie shouted. "She's going to barf!"

My hands were on my stomach. I fought to keep my mouth shut.

"She'll ruin the ice!" Jamie said. "Quick, get her off!"

"No!" I tried to say, because team captains do not throw up.

"I'll help her." I looked down and there was Aristotle, tugging on my sleeve.

The rink began to spin. I shook off Aristotle's hand. "Leave me alone!" I tried to say, as bright red secret power juice came gushing from my mouth.

Later that night, I went over to Georgie's house. I stood on his porch for a long time before I made myself knock. Finally, Georgie opened the door and said, "You've been standing there forever. What do you want?"

"Revenge," I said. Okay, whispered.

Georgie blinked at me. "Revenge?"

"On Jamie," I said.

"Oh!" he said. "Revenge on Jamie." He leaned against the door frame. "She is pretty rude. After you left, the rink manager made us get off the ice so they could clean it up. Jamie kept talking about how stupid you were to throw up."

"I didn't want to throw up!" I cried.

"I know," Georgie said. "You don't have to yell."

"Sorry," I said. I sat down on the porch steps.

Georgie sat down beside me. "It's not that big a deal. My dad was only a little bit mad."

I wrapped my arms around my knees and squeezed them tight. "Your dad was mad?"

"Oh yeah," Georgie said. "He really wanted that practice time, because there's only two practices left before our first game, and he says we don't have any reliable scorers except for Jamie. He asked me if I wanted to practice shooting this weekend, but I said no."

"I'm going to be a reliable shooter," I said. "You could be too. We have to think like a torpedo like Max said."

Georgie snorted. "That torpedo thing's not going to work."

"Yes, it is," I said.

He shook his head. "Thinking like a torpedo is not going to make me any better at hitting the puck with that weenie little stick."

"It will!" I said. "You have to give it a try. Max is in high school. He knows way more things than you. He's practically a hockey professional."

"You know," Georgie said, as if he didn't want to talk about Max anymore, "Jamie is kind of a girly-girl."

"She's a total girly-girl!" I said. "She likes to wear skirts and nail polish, and her hair is always poofy."

Georgie leaned back on his elbows and turned his head. I could practically see his thoughts bubbling. "Girly-girls don't like gross things."

"Yeah," I said. "They don't. Stuff like worms and slime —"

Georgie nodded. "And bugs and snails."

"And slugs," I said. I sat up very straight. Every part of me was going tingly. Slugs. I stood up. There was an army of slugs in my backyard just waiting to be revenge. "Thanks!" I said, walking down the steps. "That's a great idea."

Georgie stood up too. He climbed the porch steps, then opened the door and looked at me one more time. "Good luck," he said. "I think you're going to need it."

"It'll be great!" I said. "See you tomorrow!" Slugs! It was perfect!

As I walked back home, another thought occurred to me: I could teach everyone on my team how to be a torpedo! Then everyone would score! Our team would go from just Jamie scoring to everyone being scoring professors.

My dad would come to my games to see something like that. He'd probably even come to my practices. I could tell him how I'd shared the torpedo idea with everyone instead of keeping it to myself, and he'd be so proud. Plus, Coach Diaz would see my efforts and make me team captain.

Monday's practice would be the best ever.

Chapter 10

Monday morning, I gave the twins their instructions. "Here," I said, handing Cale a large Tupperware. "Fill this with slugs. I need it before hockey practice this afternoon."

"Cool," Tate said.

"Awesome," Cale said. "I never thought of putting slugs in a Tupperware before. We could put slugs in everything — Mom's pots, her measuring cups!"

"After you fill up the Tupperware," I said, but they were already running outside.

I was the first member of my team to get to the rink that afternoon. Carolina was the second.

"Hi!" I said as she approached the benches. "Have you ever thought about being a torpedo?"

Carolina looked at me, shook her head, mumbled something about getting a drink, and hurried away.

So that didn't go so great.

Munion number one was the next one to arrive. I really did not want to talk to her, but if I was going to be team captain, I had to. "You know, if you think about being a torpedo while you're shooting, you'll probably score," I told her.

"You almost threw up on me," she said. Then she sat down far away.

So that didn't go so great either.

"Time to warm up!" Coach Diaz called just as I was trying to convince Quinn to meditate with me. "We're going to take turns skating down the ice and taking shots."

"I'm going to be a torpedo, Coach," I said as I skated by.

"Oh, good," he said.

My team was forming a line behind Jamie, who always had to go first. "All right, everybody!" I said. "Think like a torpedo and you'll score!"

"What's she talking about?" Jamie Redmond said as loud as she could to munion number two.

"She keeps talking about tornadoes," munion number two said. "She's so weird."

Coach blew the whistle, and Jamie took off like a tiger on the hunt. She got to the net so fast, she'd scored before I could blink. Jamie's munions went next. Both of them missed, but they got down the ice with the puck. Miranda did her best to skate down the ice — she only fell once. Georgie skated down the ice but forgot the puck. Josh skated down the ice and shot the puck right into the net. *Bam!*

Wow, I thought. *He must have thought like a torpedo!*

I was next. This was my very last chance to impress Coach. I closed my eyes and pictured myself as a torpedo, terrifying the ice. Then I opened my eyes and took off, the puck inside my stick. I had to slow down, because the puck kept trying to drift

away, but I made it to the net. *Torpedo,* I thought.
Torpedo!

"You can do it, Sylvie!" Miranda shouted.

I swung back the stick. *Torpedo, torpedo, torpedo.*

BAM! My stick smacked the ice. The puck went
a little to the left and hit my skates. Then it just sat
there, not moving.

I'd pictured myself being a torpedo, the best torpedo I could be, and it hadn't worked.

Jamie and her munions laughed.

"Next!" Coach Diaz called.

I checked the clock and skated over to Coach. "Can I go to the bathroom?" I asked.

He frowned, looked at my stick as if he wished it would do what he wanted it to do, then nodded. "Go. But be fast about it. I want you to try that again."

I hesitated, because I needed to try that again. Maybe I wasn't scaring the ice enough. But it was now or some other time for the slugs.

Georgie, spying on our conversation, raised his eyebrows at me. I raised my eyebrows back, then skated away.

Jamie caught up with me before I could get off the ice. "You close your eyes when you shoot," she said.

I turned to her aghastly. "I do not!"

"You do," she said. "I've noticed it before. Your eyes completely shut when you swing."

"No way," I said. "I know how important it is to keep your eyes open! I play baseball!"

"You play baseball?" she said.

"Very funny," I said. "Ha ha. As if you didn't —"

"Jamie!" Coach shouted. "It's your turn. Sylvie, please hurry."

Jamie skated away without even a backward glance.

"Yeah, right," I muttered as I moved off the ice. "Like you don't know I play baseball. Close my eyes, yeah, right. I don't do that. Only lame-os would do something like that."

I looked over at Jamie, whose eyes were wide open. She was just trying to make me nervous so I'd never score.

I stepped off the ice and got down on my knees. Thanks to the wall around the rink, I was out of sight. I crawled over to my things, pulled off my skates, and hid them under my bag. Then I rummaged around for the Tupperware my brothers had given me right before I left for practice. It was full to the lid with my secret weapon.

I could just walk over and tip the slugs inside Jamie's bag, but it was risky. Georgie had caught Jamie zipping up my bag when she was ruining my lotion. Her bag was leaning up against one of the metal benches near the rink, so I crawled closer. The bench would make the perfect hiding place for my mission, so I set down my slugs and squeezed beneath it.

Squeezing underneath a not-so-tall metal bench is a painful thing to do. The bench scraped the skin on my back, it bruised my kneecaps, and it nearly popped my shoulder from its joint, but you have to do things like that when something is important.

Now hidden, I pulled the Tupperware of slugs underneath the bench with me.

The whistle blew. "All right, folks!" Coach shouted. "Gather round. I've got an announcement."

Announcement! What announcement? It couldn't be team captain time. That was supposed to come at the end of practice, after Coach had seen me score at least seven times.

It's okay, I told myself. *There's still a chance you can be team captain.* But I wished I was standing on the ice next to the others. Miranda would be holding my hand. She would whisper that I would be a great team captain, but it was okay if I wasn't.

"It's been a difficult decision, picking a team captain," Coach Diaz said. "All of you could have done a great job. But in the end, there was one person who put forth such tremendous effort both on the ice and with the team, it was clear who my choice should be. This person made it to every practice. This person built up their teammates through encouragement, praise, and a willingness to share the puck. This person intuitively knew when they should be trying their best or when they should be helping other people do their best."

A drop of sweat dribbled into my eye. Coach was not talking about Jamie. She never shared the puck with anyone. What did "intuitively" mean anyway?

"And he always offered to help without promise of reward," Coach continued.

He. Coach just said "he." He could not be me because I was a she. He couldn't be Jamie either. But what boy could he be talking about?

"Josh Stetson will be the team captain this year," Coach Diaz said.

My elbows collapsed and I banged my forehead on the metal bar in front of me. *Josh?* Josh was going to be team captain?

"I'd like everyone to give Josh a hand," Coach said, as if it was perfectly normal for Josh to suddenly become team captain. "And I hope you will congratulate him."

People clapped. Georgie whooped. I think Miranda whistled. I couldn't believe it. What would my dad say? What would I tell him? Was Josh even good?

"Time for break," Coach Diaz said.

All of a sudden, I didn't want to be under that bench. I needed to be out in the sun, away from the ice, where I could think. Josh was team captain?

Two legs plopped in front of me. Jamie's legs. Her bottom made the bench creak. One of Jamie's munions sat down beside her. *Boom!* The other one sat down on the other side. *Boom!* It was a bottom earthquake.

"Are you okay?" one munion said. Not to me, to Jamie.

"Shut up," Jamie said. "I'm fine. Totally fine. I just can't believe it — him! Josh, or whatever his name is. He stinks! Our whole team stinks. He's never even played hockey before!"

"But he's best friends with Coach's son," one munion said.

"He's Coach's pet," the other munion said. "Because he's always holding his clipboard."

That wasn't fair. Josh wasn't doing that just to be team captain! He was doing that because he was Josh.

"At least he didn't choose that one girl," Jamie said.

"Tornado girl?" the other munion said. "Oh, I know. She's the worst."

"I tried to tell her why she stinks at shooting today, and she practically cried." Jamie's voice grew sharp. "This is the lamest team ever. Come on, let's go to the bathroom."

They left, one huge bottom after the other. The bench sighed in relief.

I did not. Jamie Redmond was the meanest girl in the world. How dare she talk about Josh that way!

I yanked Jamie's bag closer and pulled down the zipper. Then I pried off the Tupperware lid. The slugs were smashed so close together, they looked like one giant slug swimming in a sea of slug juice. A hundred slug tails wiggled on the surface. "At least he didn't choose that one girl," Jamie had said. "Tornado girl," her munion had said.

I took one long breath, imagined Jamie's horrible face, then dumped the slugs into her bag.

Chapter 11

Mission accomplished, all I had to do now was get out from under the bench, so I made myself as small as a slug and tried to squeeze out.

Bang! My head crashed into the underside of the bench. *Bam!* My back did the exact same thing. I couldn't seem to make myself small enough.

Maybe it'll be easier if I get my arm out first, I thought, so I stuck out my arm. That didn't help. I tried sticking out my leg, but it wouldn't go.

I was trapped.

Coach blew his whistle. "Break's over!" he called. "But before we get started again, there's one more thing I want to discuss. All ears on me, please."

The rink went silent.

"It has come to my attention that several cruel pranks have been played on members of this team."

Coach Diaz's voice was quiet, but it still seemed loud. "Pranks are a form of bullying, kids, and if this continues, the rest of the season will be canceled. For everyone. Is that understood?"

My head jerked up, banging into the bench again. I looked at Jamie's bag where the slugs were now swimming, dripping their sliminess all over her things.

"Unless the guilty person confesses," Coach continued. "Then the rest of the team can keep playing.

Now, back on the ice. Let's have a great second half of practice."

Oh no! I had to get out from beneath the bench before Jamie saw her bag. Before Coach canceled the season. I'd run home, that's what I'd do. Then I'd write Coach Diaz a letter confessing what I did so everyone else could keep playing.

That's when Jamie and one of her munions returned to the bench and sat down again.

"Do you think anyone heard me crying in there?" Jamie whispered.

"No," the munion said. "There was too much flushing. But are you too sad to play? We can go home early — I can tell Coach you don't feel good."

Jamie sniffled. "I just wish I'd been nicer to everyone. That's why he's team captain. I tried, but I'm no good at that. Is my face red?"

"A little," the munion said. "Maybe you should dump your water bottle on your head like tornado girl did. Then no one will notice."

"I don't know why she did that," Jamie said,

followed by another sniffle. "I never would. It ruined her hair."

They were acting as if they had nothing to do with my water-bottle lid, but I knew the truth! Water-bottle lids don't just unscrew themselves, and no one else on my team was out to get me. Were they?

It's okay, I thought. *Just keep breathing. You are probably hallucifying because of claustrophobia. You are probably going crazy, because everything is going wrong.*

"Jamie!" Coach Diaz called.

"Coming!" Jamie called in reply.

"Maybe the whole season will be canceled," the munion said.

"Whoever's doing those pranks better stop." Jamie leaned forward. The bench creaked. "I'm going to be so mad if hockey's over." Her hand appeared in front of me. She was grabbing her bag and pulling it closer. "Do you want a mint?" she asked the munion.

No, I thought. *Don't open your bag. Please, get back on the ice!*

Jamie unzipped her bag. She grew very quiet. Then she screamed. "Oh my gosh, oh my gosh!" She let go of her bag and kicked it away. Slugs tumbled onto the floor.

"What is that?" her munion said, leaning forward. "Oh gross!"

"They're slugs!" Jamie said. "In my bag!"

Hold very still, I told myself. But my arms and legs were trembling.

"Coach!" the munion shouted. "Somebody put slugs in Jamie's bag!"

"Shut up!" Jamie hissed. "It's another prank! He'll cancel the season!"

The munion gasped. "Never mind, Coach!" she shouted. "I was just kidding!"

But Coach Diaz was already at the bench. "What are those things — slugs?"

"It's my fault," Jamie said. "I brought a Baggie of slugs. It must have exploded."

"You brought slugs to practice?" Coach said.

"Yes?" she said with a big question mark on the end. "I — I've been collecting them?"

"Jamie," Coach Diaz said. "You aren't collecting slugs." He paused for a long time, probably to stare at her or the slugs. "This is another prank, isn't it?"

Jamie didn't say anything for a minute. Then she said, "I'm not sure."

Coach stepped closer to Jamie. "But you didn't bring these slugs to practice."

Jamie sniffled. Then her voice grew very quiet. "Okay," she said. "I didn't bring them."

I imagined Coach Diaz growing ten feet tall.

"All right," he boomed. "It's time for this nonsense to stop. I want whoever did this to admit it right now."

My hands shook on the rubbery floor. I felt dizzy and my stomach hurt. It wasn't fair. This was my first prank. Why wasn't Jamie confessing?

"Tell the truth," Coach Diaz said. "You'll be glad later. I promise."

Later. I thought about later. Later, when my dad asked how hockey practice went and I had to tell him the truth. "You ruined the whole season?" he would say. "Team captains don't do that, Sylvie! I'm so disappointed in you."

I couldn't tell the truth. But if I didn't, Miranda and Georgie and Carolina and Quinn and Ravi and Michael and that small kid, the third grader, and even the munions wouldn't get to play again. Everyone's work would be for nothing.

"It was me," I said in a voice as wobbly as a grandma's.

When no one said anything, I said it again louder. "IT WAS ME."

Jamie screamed. The munion screamed. They jumped off the bench.

Georgie groaned.

Jamie's face appeared upside down. "Sophie?" she said.

Coach Diaz's head appeared too, also upside down. "Sylvie!" he said. "What are you doing under there?"

"It was me," I said to his beard. "I put the slugs in Jamie's bag."

"Dad," Georgie said. "It wasn't Sylvie's fault."

"Someone pranked her lots of times," Miranda said. "They unscrewed the lid to her water bottle, they put mayonnaise in her lotion, and they blew baby powder on her while she was in the bathroom."

"Baby powder?" Josh said. "Is that what it was?"

"Thank you," Coach said quietly. "But this is serious, and I need to talk to Sylvie. I believe she's trapped under there. Help me lift up this bench, Georgie."

Jamie's been pranking me, I thought, as Georgie and Coach Diaz raised the bench so I was free. *She didn't want me to score because she wanted to be team captain. It's not fair.* But I couldn't say that out loud. It didn't sound good enough.

"I saw baby powder in your bag," I heard Josh say as Coach helped me to my feet. He was standing behind me, so I couldn't see him.

"You did?" Aristotle said.

"What do you know about this?" Coach said to Georgie.

Georgie shrugged. "I saw Jamie zipping up Sylvie's bag that day someone put mayonnaise in her water bottle."

"Lotion bottle," Miranda corrected.

"I did not!" Jamie said. "I've never even touched her bag."

Georgie shrugged again. "I thought I saw her."

"Was it you?" Josh said, but not to Jamie.

Jamie poked me in the shoulder. "Did you think I pulled those pranks on you?"

"Sylvie?" Coach Diaz said. "Is that why you did this?"

I couldn't answer. I couldn't look anyone in the face.

"Did you do the water bottle and the mayonnaise too?" Josh said.

"Alistair?" Coach Diaz said, turning in Josh's direction.

"Why would I prank *you*?" Jamie Redmond said to me, as if I were a slug.

I looked up at her, my face hot and sweaty. "Because you hate me," I said.

"What?"

"Because you hate me," I said again.

Jamie looked astonished. "I don't hate you."

"Sylvie," Josh said. "It wasn't Jamie."

"You do too," I said to Jamie. "You hate me because you thought I might be team captain, and because I'm in fourth grade and you hate fourth graders. And because I'm a better pitcher than you."

"Pitcher?" Jamie said, looking as if she'd never heard of pitchers. "You pitch?"

I couldn't believe it. Was she joking? "I'm in your league!" I said. "We played each other in the championship game. You tricked me, remember?"

"Really?" Jamie had to think about this for a minute. "Oh yeah — I think I remember you now. You were that runner on second."

"Alistair," Coach Diaz said. "Is Josh right? Did you do those things to Sylvie?"

I turned around and saw the tiny boy. His arms were crossed. His mouth was shut tight. He shook off Coach's hand and ran off toward the bathrooms, fast as a cheetah.

Everyone started talking again, but I didn't listen. I was so stupid. It had been him, Alistair, the whole time. He'd shown me to the bathroom. He'd given me the red juice. I'd thought it was Jamie, and I'd ruined everything. Jamie's bag. This practice. The whole season.

I picked up my stuff and pushed past Josh, who was saying that it was just a big mix-up, and Miranda, who was pretending not to be disappointed in me, and Georgie, who was telling his dad that the slugs might have been his idea.

"Sylvie!" Miranda called. "Come back! It's okay!"

"No, it's not!" one munion said.

"It's totally not," the other said.

I hurried to the front doors and pushed my way through. I would walk all the way home. I'd throw my hockey stuff in the Dumpster by the park. I'd tell my parents I didn't like hockey anymore and I wanted to quit. I'd take my life savings and buy Jamie a new bag. The end. My dad would never have to know the truth.

"Sylvie!" my dad called.

I looked out into the parking lot and there was my dad, shutting his car door.

He was here. My bag fell from my shoulder. My legs crumpled beneath me. I sat on the ground, put my arms around my legs, and began to cry. Now he would know.

My dad lifted me up somehow and put me in the car. He asked me to explain why I was sad, but only sniffles and sobs and sadness would come.

Then Coach Diaz came out of the rink to check on me, and my dad left me alone in the car so they could talk.

They spoke in whispers I couldn't hear. Not that I wanted to hear. I didn't want to hear anything ever again.

Then the car door opened. I was too tired to cry anymore, but I squeezed my eyes tight.

"Sylvie," my dad said, and he didn't sound mad.

I opened my eyes and looked up into his face. His eyes were crinkled and his mouth hung down. He didn't look mad, but he didn't look happy. He pushed himself halfway into the car and wrapped his arms around me. My nose smashed into his chest as he hugged me tight and rocked me back and forth. I could hardly breathe, but I didn't stop him.

When he let go, I waited for a lecture, because hugs were almost always followed by lectures.

"I had a talk with your coach," he said. "And I think I understand what's been going on. I think —

I think maybe it's time for me to give you some special help. How would you like that?"

"I didn't make team captain," I said, looking at my dad's shiny shoes, the new ones he'd bought when he got his promotion.

"I do not care if you are team captain," my dad said. "Not one bit." He stood up then and pulled me out of the car, wrapping one arm around me so I stayed upright. He locked and shut the door. "Why don't we just walk home?" he said. "I feel like a good walk."

I turned to look at the car. I thought of the long time it would take to walk home. "Why were you here?" I said. Had Coach Diaz called him to come get me?

"I came to catch the last half of your practice," he said. He squeezed my hand. "I knew they were picking team captain today, and I wanted to be here."

"So you could see me win," I said.

"So I could be with you either way," he said.

Chapter 12

I told my dad the whole story while we walked home. When I was through, he said he didn't know if I would be able to play hockey this season, but he promised everything would work out in the end. I didn't know what he meant by that, but it sounded nice.

I was in my room that night when the doorbell rang. I was supposed to be making a plan for apologizing to Jamie since I'd ruined her bag, but instead I was sitting at my window, staring across the street at Miranda's house. I could see her inside, talking to her mom. She looked happy and normal, like a person who could still play hockey.

"Sylvie," my dad said a few moments later. He had opened the door without knocking. One small head appeared beneath his. Another small head appeared next to the other. The twins. Another small head appeared next to my dad's. Ginny. He was holding her up in the air, probably to make me smile.

"Mad Max is down-stairs!" Cale hissed in a loud whisper Max could probably hear.

"And he's got a dwarf with him!" Tate added.

My dad cleared his throat at the twins. "This small boy, who I believe is Max's brother, looks pretty miserable, Sylvie. I think he'd like to apologize. And I think you ought to let him."

It must be Alistair. Was he Max's brother? He'd said he had a brother who played hockey. How had I missed that? I looked down at my quilt and the stray orange thread that was still out of place. "Okay," I said.

My dad smiled. He rocked Ginny back and forth so that she smiled too, and I couldn't help myself. I had to smile as well. My dad plopped Ginny's head next to mine as I walked by, so she could slobber on my cheek. "Dad!" I said.

His smile got bigger. "That's my terrific big sister."

I couldn't help but smile a little more.

"Hi," I said to the floor when I got to the front entryway. I didn't want to look at Max. I'd drunk his juice when he'd told me not to. I was a failure at torpedoing. I didn't want to look at Alistair either. I wasn't mad — I just didn't want to see him.

Max cleared his large, high-school throat. "Alistair has something to say."

"I'm sorry," Alistair said. "I just — I just, I don't know — I just —"

"Wanted your attention," Max said.

I looked up then. Alistair scowled at Max, and Max scowled back.

"It's okay, Aristotle," I said.

He turned his scowl on me. "See!" he said. "You don't even know my name!"

"Alistair!" I said. "That's what I meant. Alistair. I'm sorry — it's a confusing name."

Max nodded. "People are always getting it wrong."

"People who don't like me," Alistair said to his feet.

I looked at Alistair's feet. He had on two different sneakers. One of them didn't have shoelaces. He was a strange kid, but that was okay. "I like you," I said. "I mean, I don't like-like you. But I regular-like you."

"You don't," Alistair said. "You think I'm too

small. You think I'm dumb because I'm in third grade."

Well, that really chapped my hive. "That's not true! I don't care what grade you're in!"

"You do," Alistair said. "You bring it up all the time."

"I never —" I stopped speaking before I could finish. I could hear my voice saying it: *"You're a third grader." "You're in third grade." "Fourth graders do it all the time."* I'd even told him at our first practice that third graders couldn't play hockey. Actually, I'd called him a second grader.

"I'm sorry," I said. "I didn't mean it. Not that way."

But the minute I said this, I knew it wasn't true. I had meant it. I hadn't wanted to hang out with him because he was younger than me. I was just like Jamie Redmond.

I, Sylvie Scruggs, was a third-grade-ist.

Alistair looked like he felt invisible. He looked like the way I felt around Jamie.

"It's okay that you're in third grade," I said with firmness. "There's nothing wrong with third graders. All grades are good. All grades are important. I was in third grade just last year."

Alistair stared at me, like he couldn't believe I was talking.

"You can hang out with us whenever you want," I said.

His face lit up like an electrified lion. "Really?"

"Sure," I said, and if Georgie gave me any grief about it, I'd remind him that we were not snooty fourth graders. We were no-graders — people who didn't care what grade you were in.

I stayed in the front entryway after Max and Alistair left. I knew what I had to do now. I needed be brave like Alistair. I needed to go to Jamie's house and apologize.

But I couldn't. I had been mean to Alistair. Really mean. I deserved what I got for ignoring him. But Jamie hadn't done a thing to me. She'd barely even known I existed.

I would write Jamie a note and include the money for a new bag. I would give the money and the note to Miranda to give to Jamie. Then Jamie could forget about me again.

In my room, I got out a piece of paper and a pencil and tried to think of something to say. I wanted to sound mature and grown-up. I wanted to make Jamie not hate me so much.

But all I could think of to write was, "I'm sorry."

Chapter 13

I had to go to school the next day. School was not optional, my mom said. "Even when your life has been ruined and you think everyone is talking about you. It won't be as bad as you think, Sylvie."

"It won't," my dad said, giving me another hug. He'd given me a thousand since he walked me home. "No one cares about dumb stuff like that."

I sighed. Elementary school was different when my parents were little. I've read all the Patty on the Plains books. Kids were nice back in the olden days. They played stickball in the front yard, made friends with grumpy neighbors who were really just lonely, and ate homemade cinnamon rolls every day. But times had changed. People didn't forget stupid mistakes anymore. They talked about them on the

news and on their cell phones and on the computer. They talked about them all the time.

I walked the halls with my head down, staring at my shoelaces. I sat with my friends at lunch, where we talked about molting cockroaches and not much else. None of the fifth graders spoke to me, especially not Jamie Redmond. *That's good,* I thought. But it didn't feel good.

When I saw Alistair in the hall in the afternoon, I waved at him, said his name briskly, and invited him to play baseball with us after school. Alistair was so stunned, he couldn't speak, but he came over to my house after school and we played.

Wednesday and Thursday were mostly the same. Things were sort of normal with a bit of uckiness hanging over everything.

Coach Diaz called my house on Thursday night. "Have you apologized to Jamie yet?" he asked.

"Kind of," I said. Miranda had given Jamie my note and most of my life savings — thirty-five dollars.

"Well, Josh and I have talked," Coach Diaz said. "And we decided you ought to still be allowed to play. We're also going to let Alistair continue play-ing. Would you like to remain on the team?"

I closed my eyes. I imagined myself at the rink, gliding around the ice, going faster and faster, the puck inside my stick. I was coming up on the net. Now was my time to score. But before the Sylvie in my mind could shoot, my vision faded, and I real-ized something.

I loved to play hockey, even though I was terrible with the puck. It didn't matter that I wasn't team captain. I would miss it.

"Sylvie?" Coach Diaz said. "What do you think?"

"No," I said. If Jamie didn't hate me before, she must hate me now. "I shouldn't play."

"Are you sure?" Coach said.

No, I thought. "Yes," I said.

By the end of lunch on Friday, I was ready to go home. I was tired of remembering that my friends had hockey practice after school. Even Georgie looked sorry for me. I stood up from the table to throw my Nacholicious hot lunch away.

"I heard you're quitting the team," Jamie Redmond said.

I jumped in surprise. Then I took a deep breath and looked right at her. "I'm sorry I ruined your bag."

"You already told me that," Jamie said. "Besides, I went shopping yesterday and bought a new bag with your money. I like it even better than my old one." She waved her perfectly nail-polished hand in my face. "You can't quit the team."

"What?" I said, because I had to be hallucifying again.

"You are not quitting the team," she said again.

"I have to," I said. "I've already told Coach."

Jamie crossed her bossy arms. "Well, I say you can't. We need you, and if you'd keep your eyes open when you shoot, you'd start scoring. We're playing the best team in the league next week. Come to practice today."

I looked down at my lunch and tried to think. Did I close my eyes when I tried to hit the puck? I didn't know. But Jamie wanted me on the team. "I don't think —" I began.

"You have to be there," she said. Her eyeballs overpowered mine. "You will be there."

"Okay," I squeaked.

With a sharp nod, she walked away.

Kids swirled around me with their own Nacho-licious lunches. Globs of yellow cheese dripped onto the floor. Jamie wasn't mad. She thought I was good at hockey, even though I was in fourth grade. She wanted me to play.

Chapter 14

It was the first game of the season. Our team was down 2–1, and we only had five minutes left to play. Coach called a time out. "Get the puck to Jamie or Josh," he said to us.

"We can't," Georgie said. "They're guarding them all the time. They'll only steal it and score."

Coach scowled. He looked at our team. His eyes landed on me. "Get the puck to Sylvie."

"Me?" I said. "Coach — I can't do it. I've never made it into the net."

"You can do it," Josh said.

"Just keep your eyes open," Jamie said.

Coach nodded. "Now go out there and finish this game by giving it your best effort!"

We stuck our sticks in the middle of our huddle. "Go!" we shouted. Then we tried to break away, but it didn't work, because our sticks were tangled together.

"Sylvie!" someone called.

I looked up into the stands, and there was Max. "You need to watch the puck!" he said. "You close your eyes whenever you shoot."

"But I can't!" I cried. "I've been trying to think like a torpedo like you said!"

"A torpedo?" Max said, blinking. "Did I tell you that?"

"Yes!" I said. "It's your big secret!"

Coach pointed at the center of the rink. "They're about to start the clock, Sylvie."

"That was just a theory," Max shouted. "Keep your eyes open, and you'll be great."

The whistle blew. I skated out on the ice, more confused than ever. A theory? What did he mean by that?

The puck went back and forth down the ice. I did a good job skating fast and keeping up on defense, but every time the puck came close, I stayed away. I was too afraid to try.

After a minute, there was a penalty and the other team missed a free shot. We lined up in position with two minutes left to play. I looked up at my family, watching me with big, excited eyes. The twins held a poster meant to encourage and inspire me.

I looked at the boy standing across from me. He looked mean, like he wanted to drink my blood. I looked at Jamie, who was glancing over her shoulder from her position as center forward. She nodded at me. I gulped, but nodded back. She was going to give me the puck.

The ref blew the whistle — *whack!* Jamie hit the puck, and — oh my goodness — it came right at me. I wanted to duck, but I made myself look. I forced my eyes open and I hit it — *pabam!* Jamie grabbed the puck with her stick. She shot off down the ice, Josh beside her. They hit the puck back and forth to each other, moving faster than the other team, but just barely.

"Go, Sylvie!" Miranda called from behind me. She was playing goalie. She'd been doing a great job. "Go help!"

So I did. Like a leopard chasing prey through the jungle, I took off after Josh and Jamie.

"Sylvie!" Josh shouted. He had the puck. He was about to pass it to me.

He was surrounded. Jamie was surrounded. I was open. I shook my head. I couldn't do it. I could practically feel my eyes shutting. But Josh was already hitting the puck in my direction. There was nothing I could do.

Eyes open! I ordered myself, and even though the puck was coming so fast I could hardly see it, I kept my eyes open, as wide as they could go. I lifted my stick over my shoulder. I swung it forward. *Keep them open!* I thought.

Whack!

BEEP!

Oh my gosh! I'd scored!

"Time's up, ladies and gentlemen," the announcer man announced. "After that last-minute goal, we have a tie, two to two. Congratulations on a great game for both teams, the Tomcats and the — wait a second, is this right?"

There was some muffled whispering.

"Are you sure?" the announcer man said. "All right then. Congratulations also go to the

No-Graders! Put your hands together for these two terrific teams."

Alistair skated up to give me the biggest high five of his life. "Good game," I told him.

"Nice shot," he said with his mouth full of his mouthpiece.

"You did it, Sylvie Scruggs!" Max shouted from the bleachers.

I looked up in the stands to find my dad. There he was with my mom and the twins and Ginny. They were all clapping, even Ginny with the help of my mom.

"Good job, sweetie!" my dad shouted. "I knew you could do it!"

Jamie Redmond slapped her glove hard on my back. After I fell over, she reached out to help me up. "Way to keep your eyes open, Sophie," she told me.

"Thanks," I said.

Sylvie Scruggs's Rules for Being a No-Grader

- Remember that you were once in the grade below you — unless you skipped a grade.
- Smile with big teeth at people who are younger than you are. Unless it makes them cry.
- If someone seems small, look at them again with a telescope.
- Never tell small people that they can't do something because they're small. Except for driving.
- Say this to anyone younger than you: "I really like younger people. Your bones might be smaller, but they are exactly the same shape!"
- If you don't know how to treat a younger person, just ask yourself how you would have

liked an older person to treat you when you were younger. This is a confusing rule, but it's important.

- If someone asks you what grade you're in, say, "I'm in the grade of life," then wiggle your eyebrows mysteriously.
- When people are rude to you about your grade, sniff and say, "I smell rotten pinecones." Then walk away while they look for rotten pinecones.
- Don't judge people by their grade level. Or their grades. Or their levels.
- Be friends with everyone, because you never know when your twin brothers might start your house on fire and you'll need a new place to live.

ABOUT THE AUTHOR

Lindsay Eyre is a mother of five, a graduate of the MFA program in Creative Writing at the Vermont College of Fine Arts, and a fanatical lover of books. She lives in the grand but sweaty city of Cary, North Carolina. Please visit her website at www.lindsayeyre.com and follow her at @LindsayEyre.

ABOUT THE ILLUSTRATOR

Sydney Hanson grew up in Minnesota with numerous pets and brothers. She is the illustrator of *D Is for Duck Calls*, by Kay Robertson, and now lives in Los Angeles. Please visit her website at sydwiki.tumblr.com.

This book was edited by Cheryl Klein and designed by Nina Goffi and Carol Ly. The production was supervised by Elizabeth Krych. The text was set in Bembo, with display type set in Futura. The book was printed and bound by CG Book Printers in North Mankato, Minnesota. The manufacturing was supervised by Shannon Rice.